Teena Tortoise

HAPPY READING!

This book is especially for:

_____

Suzanne Tate
Author—
brings fun and
facts to us in her
Nature Series.

James Melvin
Illustrator—
brings joyous life
to Suzanne Tate's
characters.

Suzanne and James with a new friend

Teena Tortoise
A Tale of a Little Giant

Suzanne Tate
Illustrated by James Melvin

Nags Head Art

To Gladys
(1944-2011)
a shining star on earth
now lighting up the heavens

Library of Congress Control Number 2011914510
ISBN 978-1-878405-60-9
ISBN 1-878405-60-8
Published by
Nags Head Art, Inc., P.O. Box 2149, Manteo, NC 27954
Copyright© 2011 by Nags Head Art, Inc.

Teena Tortoise was a little giant.
She was a young, giant tortoise.

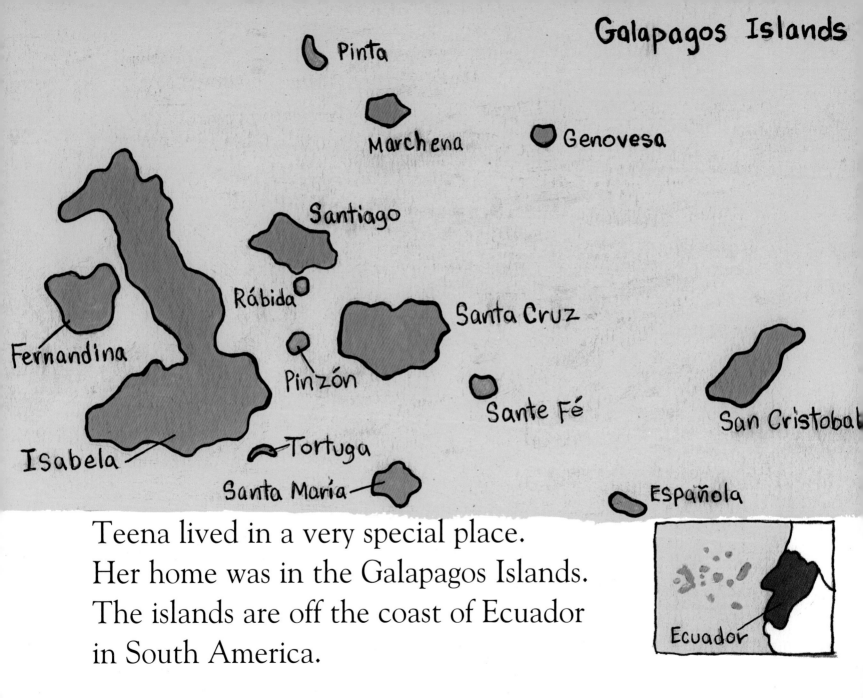

Teena lived in a very special place.
Her home was in the Galapagos Islands.
The islands are off the coast of Ecuador
in South America.

Animals and birds in the Galapagos Islands
are not afraid of anybody. They don't run away
or fly when someone comes near.

Teena Tortoise began life at a busy place called
the Charles Darwin Research Station.
She hatched from an egg and was cared for
so she would be safe.

"I'm glad that HELPFUL HUMANS
help little giants like me," she thought.
"But I wish I could go out and
see more of the world."

Teena sighed and decided
to be patient.
She was, after all, never hungry
and always safe.

One day, HELPFUL HUMANS decided
that she was big enough to be on her own.

Teena was excited!
She was taken to a place where
she could see larger tortoises.

At first, Teena was afraid.
A great big giant tortoise was there
holding his head up high.

"He looks scary!" she thought.

But another large tortoise
was friendly to her.

"That's Uncle Henry," she said to Teena.
"Don't be afraid of him — he just
wants to be the boss of all of us."

Teena crawled up beside her.
"I don't know where my mother is.
May I call you Auntie?"

"Oh, yes, you may call me Auntie,"
the big tortoise replied.
"Here, try these green blades of grass
— you will like them."

"Thank you," Teena said as she munched some green grass.
"Will you tell me now about this place where we live?"

"Are there other creatures here besides us?" she asked.

"Oh, yes," Auntie replied.
"Many animals and birds live in
the Galapagos Islands.
They are different from any
other place in the world."

"How do you know about these things?"
Teena asked.

"An old giant tortoise named
Lonesome George told me.
He is over 100 years old,"
Auntie said.

"But Lonesome George isn't lonesome.
HELPFUL HUMANS put him
in a nice place with a pool of water.
Two friends keep him company."

"There used to be 200,000 giant tortoises
living in these islands.
Now there are only about 15,000,"
Auntie went on to say.

"What happened to them?"
Teena asked.

"In olden days, many tortoises were taken away on ships," Auntie replied. "A big tortoise can live for a year without food or water."

"Sailors on the ships used them for food," Auntie said.
"Oh, my," Teena sighed.
"That's really scary!"

"Tell me now about birds," Teena said.
"Do a lot of birds live on these islands?"

Red-footed
Booby

Nazca
Booby

Swallow-tailed
Gull

Flightless
Cormorant

Great
Blue
Heron

"Oh, yes, Lonesome George says
the birds here are fantastic!
There are many different kinds."

"One is called a blue-footed booby," Auntie said.
"It likes to show off its
bright blue feet!"

"The blue-footed booby is a great fisherman.
It dives straight down from the sky
to catch fish deep down in the water."

"Lonesome George says that a little
blue-footed booby is such fun to watch."

"The young bird tosses a stick up in the air
and has fun catching it over and over."
"I wish I could see that,"
Teena said.

"Then there are big frigate birds.
They spend most of their lives
flying over the ocean," Auntie said.
"Sometimes, they are called pirate birds."

"Why is that?" Teena asked.
"They are called pirates because they steal
food from other birds," Auntie replied.

"Lonesome George says it is amazing to see
frigate birds trying to attract mates.
They puff themselves up in front like red balloons,
wave their heads and call to females flying above."

"There are many other birds living in these islands," Auntie said. "Among them are lively penguins, perky pelicans and pretty flamingos."

"What about other animals
living here?" asked Teena.

"You can see lots of lizards lying together
to get warm," replied Auntie.
"They are called marine iguanas."

"The iguanas are cold and must warm up after fishing in the ocean for seaweed," Auntie explained.

"Colorful animals called sally-lightfoot crabs join them on the black rocks."

"Colonies of sea lions rest on the beaches," she said.
"The young sea lions are often lively,
playing games and body surfing."
"I would like to see them," Teena thought.

"There is truly a wondrous world of nature in the Galapagos Islands," Auntie went on to say.

— work to keep it that way!

"I'm glad we have them," Teena Tortoise said. "I hope that HELPFUL HUMANS will be here forever."